Carl the Complainer

by Michelle Knudsen
illustrated by Maryann Cocca-Leffler

Kane Press, Inc.
New York

Library of Congress Cataloging-in-Publication Data

Knudsen, Michelle.
  Carl the complainer / by Michelle Knudsen ; illustrated by Maryann Cocca-Leffler.
    p. cm. — (Social studies connects)
  Summary: Carl and his friends embark on a plan to make the town council extend the hours the park is
open.
  ISBN 1-57565-157-2 (alk. paper)
  [1. Parks—Fiction. 2. City and town life—Fiction.] I. Cocca-Leffler, Maryann, 1958- ill. II. Title. III.
Series.
  PZ7.K7835Car 2005
  [E]—dc22
                                    2005004553

10 9 8 7 6 5 4 3 2 1

First published in the United States of America in 2005 by Kane Press, Inc.
Printed in Hong Kong.

Social Studies Connects is a trademark of Kane Press, Inc.

Book Design: Edward Miller

www.kanepress.com

My friends say I complain a lot. They even call
me Carl the Complainer.

But hey, some things are just so annoying!

Like TV jingles that get stuck in your head. And
paper cuts. And mint chocolate-chip ice cream
that's not the right shade of green.

It's five o'clock—the time the town park closes. I get a drink on the way out. "Water fountain water is never cold enough," I tell my friend Dale.

"Look on the bright side," he says. "At least it's wet!"

Dale always looks on the bright side. It's really annoying.

"Five P.M. is way too early for the park to close," I complain for about the millionth time. Dale rolls his eyes. "If it really bothers you, maybe you should try to do something about it— instead of just complaining all the time."

PARK CLOSES
AT 5 P.M.
Hanford Town Council

We turn down Dale's street. "At least we've *got* a town park," he goes on. "Look—"

"I know, I know," I say, laughing. "Look on the bright side!"

Dale starts laughing.

"Keep it down out there!" Dale's next-door neighbor yells.

"Sorry, Mr. Henry," we both call out.

We go into Dale's house.

I show Dale a cool website. But an ad pops up—then four more. "Pop-up ads are so annoying," I complain. I start clicking them all closed.

"Wait!" says Dale. "There's a petition to save *Power Friends!* I want to sign it. I love that show."

"Why bother?" I say. "The best shows always get canceled. It's so annoying."

"That's what the petition is about," Dale explains. "If the network sees that lots of kids like the show, they might keep it on."

POWER FRIENDS is in **DANGER** of going off the air! Sign this petition **NOW** to show you want more thrilling POWER FRIENDS adventures!

"Can anyone start a petition?"

Dale shrugs. "Sure, I guess. Why?"

"Maybe *we* should start one," I say. "A petition to keep the park open later!"

"Great idea!" Dale says. "But how do we do it?"

A **petition** is a written request. People sign a petition to show that they agree with the request. Many petitions are on the Internet, and some are passed around by hand.

We look at each other. We don't have a clue.
"There's always the Internet," says Dale.
A few clicks later, we find a how-to site about petitions.

PERFECT PETITION POINTERS

1. Give it a title (for example, "Petition to Make Bigfoot the New School Mascot").
2. Say whom it is addressed to.
3. Say who is sending it.
4. Say what you want to do or change.
5. Get people to sign it—the more people, the better!
6. Give it to a person or group who has the power to do what you want to get done.

Dale points to number 6. "Who decides about the park's hours?"
"I don't know," I tell him.
So we go to the park and check out the sign.

"Hanford Town Council," I read. "What's that?"

A woman hears me and turns around. "It's a group of people who decide things for the town," she says.

We tell her about our petition, and she tells us that we have to talk at a council meeting!

"There's one next week," she adds.

PARK CLOSES
AT 5 P.M.
Hanford Town Council

Dale and I write up the petition and make copies. Then we get our friends together and tell them about our plan.

"I'll help collect signatures," says Laura.

"Me, too!" adds Tony. "It would be great if the park stayed open later."

Mary and Pete want to help, also!

We all take copies and split up into teams.

Petition to Change Park Hours

To: Hanford Town Council

We, the following community members of Hanford, would like the town park to stay open later. We feel the kids of Hanford need a good place to play baseball (and other things). Grown-ups could stay in the park later, too.

My parents are happy to sign. "That's two names already," I say. "This will be a snap!"

But Mrs. Monroe next door says, "Sorry, kids, now isn't a good time."

At the next house, Mr. Adams listens to about one sentence. "Not interested," he mumbles.

So we were hoping—

"Maybe we should try some place with more people," I suggest.

"How about the mall?" Dale says. So that's where we go.

"Want to sign our petition?" I ask a friendly looking girl.

"Are you giving away free stuff?" she replies.

"Uh, no," I say.

"Oh. I thought you were." She walks away.

People have been writing petitions for thousands of years. Scientists have even found petitions in the tombs of ancient Egyptians.

We try the train station.

We try the supermarket.

But most people are too busy to even listen to what we have to say.

We all meet up at Dale's. Nobody's had much luck. "This is so annoying," I groan.

"There *must* be more people who want the park open later," says Laura.

"That's it!" I shout. "We should be talking to people at the park!"

"Yesssss!" everybody yells.

"Quiet down out there!" Mr Henry booms.

"We'd better go inside and start on Plan B," Dale whispers.

In the 1830's, many Americans signed petitions to the U.S. government asking that slavery be stopped in the United States.

We sit around Dale's kitchen table and start brainstorming.

"I'll bake cookies to give away," says Tony. "People will come for the cookies, and then we'll tell them about the petition!"

"Great!" says Pete. "I'll make lemonade."

"We'll need signs, too," Mary chimes in.

Dale grabs some markers, and we get to work.

We set up in the park early Saturday morning.
The signs look great. Lots of people stop at the
tables. They eat cookies. They drink lemonade.
And most of them sign the petition!

By six o'clock we have ninety-nine signatures. "If we could just get one more, we'd have an even hundred," I say. "Who haven't we asked?"

Please sign our petition.

Every American has the right to petition the government. This right is guaranteed by the First Amendment to the Constitution!

"There's always Mr. Henry," says Dale. "But—"
"Good thinking!" I tell him. "Let's go!"
"But—" Dale repeats.
I lead the way to Mr. Henry's house.

No one wants to ring the doorbell. "You should do it, Dale," says Tony. "It was your idea."

Dale gulps and presses the bell. Mr. Henry opens the door.

"Uh, hi," Dale starts. "We were wondering if maybe you would sign our petition to keep the park open later."

"The park hours are just fine," Mr. Henry growls. He starts to close the door.

"Wait!" I call out.

"Mr. Henry, you're always complaining that we make too much noise. So maybe you should help us do something about it!"

"Oh, really? Like what?" he snaps.

"You could sign our petition!" I reply. "If the park's open later, we can stay there instead of playing in the street. And by the time the park closes, we'll be so tired that we'll just want to go inside. There'd be a lot less noise!"

Mr. Henry stares at me. Dale and the other kids stare, too.

Just when I'm ready to give up, Mr. Henry smiles. "You actually have a point there, son," he says. "Tell you what. I'll sign your petition. I'll even get some folks in my writing group to sign it, too."

"You're a writer?" I ask.

"Sure. That's why I need quiet. Do you think I yell at you kids just for the fun of it?"

We end up with 108 names. "I hope that's enough," I say. "The meeting is tomorrow!"

"You'd better practice your speech," Dale says.

My heart starts pounding. "I forgot I'd actually have to get up and talk in front of everyone."

"Don't worry," Dale tells me. "You'll be great. You're the best complainer I know."

Carl's petition is going to the town council, a part of the government. But lots of petitions go to businesses and organizations—from movie studios to sports teams to ice cream stores.

25

I'm very nervous on the night of the meeting. The council is sitting in the front of the room.

First, a lady stands up and tells them that dog licenses are too expensive.

Next, a man talks about putting a traffic light on Elm Street.

Then it's my turn.

"Good luck!" whispers Dale.

Lots of real-life kids have started petitions. One second-grade class even wrote a petition that made the ladybug the official state insect of Massachusetts!

"My friends and I love the park," I say. "But it closes at five P.M. and that's *way* too early." I hold up the petition. "All the people who signed this want the park to stay open later."

"I don't know," says the man with the moustache. "Is it a good idea to have kids playing in the park after five?"

"It's better than having them run around in the street," a lady in the audience replies.

That's when I notice Mr. Henry.

"We do play outside in the street when the park closes," I say. "Sometimes the noise bothers our neighbors."

I grin at Mr. Henry. "Keeping the park open later would solve that problem, too."

Mr. Henry smiles. But the council members are still arguing.

What if they say no?

It's time for the vote. I hold my breath.

"All in favor of keeping the park open until sundown?" asks the lady with the glasses.

One by one, the council members raise their hands.

I can hardly believe it. Our petition worked! Everybody claps and cheers.

Dale gives me a high five.

"We did it!" he says. "And the best part is, now you'll have one less thing to complain about."

"Was my complaining really that bad?" I ask.

"Yup." Dale laughs. "It was—"

"I know," I say with a grin. "Really annoying!"

We can inform and persuade!

MAKING CONNECTIONS

Informing means giving people information. **Persuading** is convincing people to share your point of view. Some people—like Mr. Henry—need a little extra persuading!

You inform and persuade all the time. Maybe you tell your parents about a movie you want to see, and convince them to take you to it. That's informing and persuading!

Look Back

- Look at page 21. How does Dale inform Mr. Henry about the petition?
- On page 22, what does Carl do to persuade Mr. Henry to sign the petition?
- Read page 27. How does Carl inform the town council about his idea?
- On page 29, how does he persuade the council to accept the petition? Why do you think this works?

Try This!

Write a petition about something that's important to you. Perhaps you want your school to buy more playground equipment or start a school band. What information would you put in your petition? How would you persuade people to sign it? When you finish collecting signatures, what would your next step be?

Be prepared! Suppose you are told your idea is too expensive? What would you do? (Suggestion: Offer to set up a bake sale to make money.)